This book belongs to:

carina

Monster stories

FOR BEDTIME

Illustrated by
JANE LAUNCHBURY

AWARD PUBLICATIONS LIMITED

ISBN 0-86163-388-1

Copyright © 1987 Templar Publishing

First published 1987 by Century Hutchinson Children's Books

This edition published 1989 by Award Publications Limited,
Spring House, Spring Place, Kentish Town, London NW5 3BH

Printed in Singapore

CONTENTS

David
and
the Dragon

by Jane Launchbury

There was a cold north wind blowing as David started the long walk home from school. The little boy shivered, and pulled the hood of his coat down over his eyes to keep out the biting cold. He walked faster when he reached the start of the woodland path, partly to keep warm, and partly because the light was beginning to fade and he hated being in the wood when it was dark. He had a very vivid imagination, and in his mind there were horrible monsters lurking behind the creaking old trees, just waiting to pounce on him. Every crack of a breaking twig made him jump and walk a little faster. He did not dare to look over his shoulder.

David hurried along the woodland path, glancing nervously into the shadows around him. He was in the thickest part of the wood, near the middle, when he saw

an extraordinary thing. Straight ahead of him, through the tangled brambles and briars, he caught a glimpse of sparkling colours and a puff of smoke. In the fading light he couldn't be sure, but he was convinced that there was a huge scaly monster lurking in the undergrowth. David stopped in his tracks. He would have to find a different way home. There was no way that he was going anywhere near whatever it was in the bushes.

Taking a deep breath and speeding up, David turned down a tiny path made by the woodland animals. He was almost running when he saw the thing again – in fact he very nearly tripped over it! From behind an old beech tree trailed a long spiny tail covered in glistening scales. The end of the tail reached right into the middle of the path. From the other side of the tree came little puffs of smoke. There was now no doubt in David's mind. In the middle of Oakapple Wood there was a real, live, fire-breathing dragon!

9

David gulped and gave a little squeak of fright. He tried to think what the brave knights did in all the fairy tales he knew. Somehow they always seemed to be armed with magic swords and shields. Pulling the hood of his coat even further over his eyes, David picked up a big stick. It would have to do instead of a magic sword. Then he thought that perhaps if he crept past the tree very quietly, the dragon might not notice him. But just as he started to move, he tripped over his shoelace and trod heavily on the scaly tail. There was a loud yelp of pain from behind the tree.

David started to shiver all over, and his teeth began to chatter. He was rooted to the spot with terror. Then above the sound of his own teeth chattering, he heard another sound. Someone else's teeth were chattering too.

"Whoever it is must have lots of teeth," thought David. Then, out of the corner of his eye, he saw something appear round the edge of the beech tree. It was the end of a thin green and yellow snout and there were little plumes of smoke rising from its nostrils.

David pulled the edges of his hood so tightly together that he could only peep out through a tiny crack.

He watched with terrified fascination as more of the snout appeared. The noise of chattering teeth got louder. David gasped in surprise as he realised what that meant – the dragon was just as frightened as he was. All its teeth were chattering, and there must have been at least

10

a hundred of them! Then a pair of very frightened orange eyes peeped around the edge of the tree.

David opened the crack in his hood a little wider, and for a long time he and the dragon looked at each other nervously. Gradually their teeth stopped chattering, although the dragon was still shivering gently. Very slowly, David pushed back the hood of his coat and smiled shyly at the dragon. It grinned in the best way that a dragon can, and David gave a little giggle. Instead of the great sharp teeth he had been expecting, the dragon had tiny rounded teeth like shiny white pearls. It was still very young and hadn't got its proper teeth yet.

Very slowly, so as not to frighten the boy, the young dragon crept out from behind the tree. It had short stumpy legs, with great big feet, and down its back were soft leathery spines. Tufts of ginger hair grew out of its two huge green ears which seemed several sizes too big. All over the dragon's body were shiny scales, glistening in the colours of the rainbow. A gust of icy wind blew through the trees, and David realised that the poor little dragon was cold! He took off his coat and put it over the creature's back.

"Thank you," whispered the dragon.

Then it took a deep breath and told David all about itself. It wasn't a very long story. The dragon's name was Jamie, and he had been born very late in the summer, up in the mountains to the north. Normally when autumn came, all the dragons migrated south, flying to warmer places for the winter. But, because Jamie was so small, he didn't have the strength to fly with all the others and had been left behind in the cold. He had flown as far as the wood and then run out of energy. A little tear ran down Jamie's scaly cheek as he told David how cold and frightened he had been in the wood.

David knew just how the dragon felt. He also knew

how to help Jamie. His mother's tiny cottage was only a few minutes away. Inside, the dragon would be cosy and warm. It was the only place to be on a cold, dark night like this. David's mother had a kind heart, and loved all the woodland animals. He was sure that she would take pity on the little creature.

David led the small, shivering dragon through the wood. As they came in sight of his home, Jamie already looked a great deal happier. David's mother was enchanted with the dragon, who was very polite and well mannered. She let him curl up in the best chair in front of the fire, and busied herself making a pot of rich, creamy soup and special biscuits.

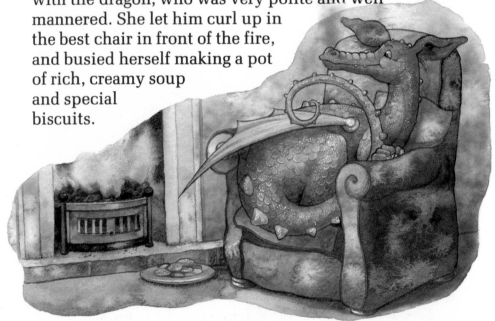

The days went by, and Jamie lost his bewildered, sad look and began to get stronger. He stayed with David and his mother throughout that long, cold winter, and every night he told them a different story – for dragons have very vivid imaginations and are wonderful storytellers.

Spring came and the evenings got lighter. Jamie sat outside the cottage, looking up into the sky. Then one day the dragon saw what he had been waiting for – his family were heading back to the mountains for the summer. Cheerfully, he unfurled his wings, and with whoops of delight, rose gracefully into the sky. Then all the dragons swooped low over the tiny cottage calling out their thanks to David and his mother before heading off to their summer home in the mountains.

For many years afterwards David watched the skies for the migrating dragons every time that spring arrived, but he never saw any of them again. Though sometimes he fancied that he could hear their gentle voices calling "Hello" on the wind that blew down from the mountains. Then he realised just how lucky he was to have met a real, live dragon as nice as Jamie had been – for, after all, not many people do these days, do they?

THE END

Prince Fanshaw's Special Monster

by Deborah Tyler

Once upon a time, for that is how all proper fairy stories begin, there was a prince. His name was Prince Fanshaw and his parents, Queen Matilda and King Bruno the Wonderful, ruled over the land of Mordinia. They were happy, but they had a problem – the Prince would not marry! They had given hundreds of balls, concerts and parties in his honour. Yet he had not asked a single girl to dance.

"They are so dull," complained the Prince. "I don't like any of them and I *certainly* wouldn't marry them."

"But all princes get married," said King Bruno. "It is their royal duty." So King Bruno arranged that his son should start rescuing as many fair maidens as possible in the hope he might meet one that he liked. First, Prince Fanshaw saved Princess Maribel Mont Percy from

a giant toad. "BORING!" he yawned. Then he rescued Lady Eleanor De Sax from a dragon. "TEDIOUS!" he cried.

So, in the end, the King and Queen just gave up.

One day, when he had finished rescuing Lady Gillian Hope-Jones from a particularly smelly sea monster, Prince Fanshaw decided to go for a long walk. He was sick of being a hero. In fact, he wished that everyone would leave him alone. Wherever he went, the locals would shout: "Look, there's brave Prince Fanshaw!" Or, "Long live the Mordinian monster slayer!"

Prince Fanshaw took his favourite path down the cliffs to the sea. It was a beautiful day – the sea glittered like silver foil, and the sky was a bright blue. Suddenly, for no reason at all, it stopped being a lovely day. The sea boiled and bubbled like Queen Matilda's home-made stew. The sky grew as black as a raven's wing.

"I hope it doesn't rain," said the Prince to himself. "My sword will rust up." But it did rain, very heavily, and soon huge drops were rolling down his sword buckle.

Prince Fanshaw looked around him. He saw a cave cut into the rock that he had never noticed before, and he ran down the rough path towards it. It was a cave which smelt of the sea and the wind. There was a bunch of seaweed hanging above the entrance and a sign which read:

"Please knock. No Tradespeople. Wipe your feet."

So he knocked on the side of the cave.

"Who is it?" asked a soft, girlish voice. There was something sad about it, like the rustle of sea grass.

"May I come in?" asked the Prince. "It is I, Prince Fanshaw, and it's raining jolly hard."

"Oh! You are the monster slayer?" said the voice.

"Yes," replied the Prince.

"Well then, you can't come in, for I am a monster!"

"Have you eaten any fair maidens?" asked Prince Fanshaw with a sigh. The creature within gave a gasp.

"No!" it cried in horror. "You see, I once was a maiden myself!"

"I won't hurt you," said the Prince, "but I don't quite understand. What do you mean, you used to be a maiden?"

"You had better come in and hear my story," said the small voice. So Prince Fanshaw entered the cave. It had walls with fish painted upon them and it seemed to be empty, but the same small voice spoke again from the shadows.

"Once," it began, "I was a princess. I was the Princess Floella and I lived in a lovely white castle, with fountains and peacocks. But I was very vain and very spoiled. I would not eat anything but the best chocolates and I would only wear dresses made of silk and pearls. I was very rude to everyone, especially my mother and father – I even threw food at the princes who came to court me. Then I made my great mistake. On my sixteenth birthday, I hit the court magician with a blackcurrant pie. I had aimed it at Prince Dortimand, who was in love with me, but it hit the magician instead. He was so angry he turned me into a monster, and I was immediately banished. But now I'm really very sorry for what I did," sniffed the monster. "I am no longer spoiled."

Prince Fanshaw had listened to the tale in silence.
Now he spoke up.

"Is there no cure?" he asked.

"I will only change back if a prince can love me and
marry me as I am," replied the monster. "But what
prince would marry a lizard!" And with that the creature
stepped forward out of the shadows. She was indeed a
lizard – a lizard with greenish-brown, slimy scales,
wearing a tattered white party dress and a little gold crown.
Prince Fanshaw smiled.

"Floella, you are a very special lizard," he said.
Princess Floella smiled back, showing her pointed
fangs. "So special that I want to marry you," said the
Prince. And he took her back to the castle with him.

"Father," he said. "This is Princess Floella. I want
to marry her."

The King was horrified.

"My dear boy!" he exclaimed. "You can't marry a
lizard!" At this point, the Queen fainted. There was a
great uproar in the court and the court lawyers were
summoned, but they could find nothing which stated
that it was against the law for a prince of the realm to
marry a lizard if he wanted to.

No one would believe that Floella was really a
princess. The ladies-in-waiting avoided her, and the
Queen was very rude.

"What sort of royal wedding will this be," she cried,
"with a lizard as a bride!"

Floella loved Fanshaw with all her heart. She was
deeply sorry, for his sake, that she looked like a horrible
monster. As a princess she had never, ever been sorry
for anyone. What if she did not change back to a

princess after the wedding and he remained married to a lizard all his life? And the more she thought, the more she worried until, one day, she decided to run away.

On the night before her wedding, Floella packed a small bag and tried to leave the castle. As she passed the castle fountain she shed two tears. Two diamond drops rolled down her scaly skin. Suddenly, she felt herself shudder and heard a crack like glass breaking. Then she heard Prince Fanshaw's voice.

"Floella, where are you going?" he cried.

"I can't marry you," she sighed. "I love you too much to see you married to a lizard." Then she looked at the ground. There, on the floor, was her lizard skin!

"No!" Fanshaw exclaimed. "You are beautiful! Look into the fountain pool."

22

Princess Floella looked into the pool. The lizard scales had gone and a beautiful girl looked up at her. She had creamy-white skin, lovely amber eyes and a mass of dark curly hair. The only sign that she had ever been a lizard was a streak of green through one of her curls. Floella wept for joy.

The wedding of Prince Fanshaw and Princess Floella was a very merry occasion. The castle and cathedral were decorated with garlands of roses and beautiful sea shells. And the children of the land hung paper fish from all the trees. Floella and Fanshaw were very happy together. They ruled their kingdom wisely and well, and in time they had a son. He was a handsome boy with golden hair – and eyes as green as a lizard.

THE END

The Storm Monster

by Gina Stewart

Peter lay in his bed in the little room under the eaves at the top of the house. He should have been fast asleep by now, but something had woken him up. He listened for a while and heard the sound of the waves beginning to crash and pound on the beach close to his home, and a moaning and a creaking as the tall pines in the forest swayed in the wind.

Peter's heart began to beat a little faster. He didn't know whether to feel excited or scared, but he knew for certain that somewhere out at sea a tremendous storm was brewing, and that it was moving in the direction of his home.

All night the tempest raged, thundering and buffeting against the house as though it meant to tear it down stone by stone. At last, when it was almost

morning, the wind dropped, giving way to a grey, cloudy, rainy day.

"There'll be lots of things blown in on the tide," said Peter at breakfast time. "*Please* may I go to the beach and see?"

"All right, Peter," said his mother with a smile. So Peter put on his anorak and wellington boots and ran down the stony path to the beach.

"Wow!" he said as he reached the sand. He had never seen the beach looking like this before. Everywhere he looked there was driftwood and seaweed, bottles and plastic containers, wooden planks and ... and ... Peter couldn't believe his eyes. There, lying upside-down near some rocks was a green wooden rowing-boat.

"Oh, thank you, storm!" said Peter. "It's just what I've always wanted."

Peter ran across the sand towards the little boat. He was just pulling some of the strands of seaweed away from the hull, when a dreadful groan stopped him in his tracks.

25

"Help!" the groan seemed to say. "Please help me!"

Peter realized that the sound was coming from underneath the boat. Although the voice was saying words that Peter understood, it wasn't like a human voice, but deep and gurgly and rather frightening. Peter was about to run back to fetch his father when the strange voice spoke again.

"Please don't go!" it said. "I can't breathe and I'm dying of thirst!"

Gathering all his strength together, Peter started tugging and heaving at the boat, but all he could do was lift one side enough to prop a small rock underneath the edge so that air could get in.

"That's ... that's a little better," gasped the voice. "Thank you ..."

"That's all right," said Peter and he knelt down by the boat and peered underneath. It took a moment for his eyes to get used to the darkness, but when they did he jumped back in terror.

For underneath the boat was a monster, a huge creature with a great round head and enormous, sad eyes.

"Please could you get me some water!" it said unhappily. "My throat's full of sand!"

Peter ran off along the beach and soon found a plastic box with rainwater in it. Carefully, he picked up the container and went back to the boat. As he passed the plastic box under the edge, two strange long arms shot out and grabbed it. There was a long gurgling noise, followed almost immediately by a violent spitting sound.

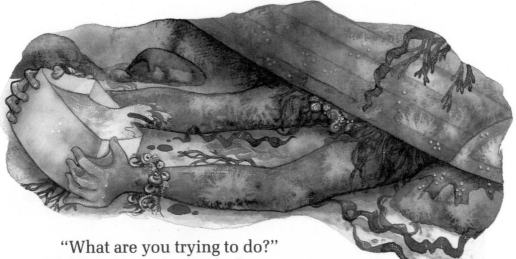

"What are you trying to do?" said the creature under the boat. "Poison me?"

"Why? What do you mean?" asked Peter.

"This is *fresh* water!" cried the monster in disgust.

"Oh, I see!" said Peter, quickly refilling the box from a nearby rock pool. "Is this what you wanted?"

While the creature drank several containers of salt water, one after the other, Peter sat and stared at it, wondering how it came to be there.

As if reading his thoughts, the monster said:

"My home is at the bottom of the farthest ocean, but I was caught on the surface when that terrible storm blew up last night. Of course, once I was in shallow water I couldn't swim, and then a tremendous wave swept me up to the top of the beach. And just when I thought I'd found a boat to float myself back to sea in, it toppled over on top of me. And here I am. Trapped. Normally I could shift a boat this size in a twinkling, but at the moment I feel rather weak."

"Can I get you anything to eat?" asked Peter.

"What have you got?" said the monster, quickly.

"Well ...," Peter peered into the rock pool. "There's seaweed, or limpets, or starfish, or shrimps ..."

"That'll do," said the monster.

"Which one?" asked Peter.

"All of them, of course!" said the monster hungrily. "And make sure the seaweed isn't all dry and nasty!"

It was easy catching the little creatures in the rock pool, and soon the monster was crunching away happily

"And while I'm eating," said the monster, with its mouth full, "you can think of a way to get me out of here."

"I am thinking," said Peter, "and I've got an idea. Tonight is the highest tide of the year," he went on, "and I'll be back then. But first you should have a rest and get your strength back."

Some hours later, when it was quite dark outside and his parents were fast asleep, Peter crept down the stairs of his house and ran down the rocky path to the beach.

"Hello, monster," he said as he reached the boat.

"You'll be pleased to hear," said the monster, "that I've managed to roll onto my back and I can now move my legs a little. Perhaps, together, we can move this boat."

At first Peter and the monster tried to lift the boat, but nothing happened. Then on the third attempt the monster, still lying on his back, gave a mighty heave. One side of the boat rose up in the air, then wobbled a little ... and then fell right way up, with a plop, onto the sand. There before Peter stood the strangest creature he had ever seen. It was blue and green – the colour of the deepest oceans – with long hair that hung like seaweed down its back. Around its head was a crown of pearly shells, and its wrists and ankles were hung with limpets and periwinkles and tiny, shiny pebbles.

"Now help me get in," said the monster, clambering into the little boat. Moments later, when the water was already lapping around Peter's feet, the sea monster was safely on board.

"There aren't any oars!" cried Peter in dismay.

But it didn't matter. The monster spread its great, long arms to their full width and, as the water lifted the boat off the sand, began paddling its way out to sea.

"Thank you!" it shouted as it vanished from sight. "Thank you, my friend!"

Next morning dawned blue, sunny and still. Peter awoke feeling sad. He knew that by now the monster would have reached deep water and would have swum down to its home at the bottom of the ocean. He would never see his new friend again.

But when he went down the stony path to the beach later that day, a marvellous sight greeted him. There, tied to a rock by a piece of seaweed, was the green rowing-boat in which the monster had paddled away the night before. And inside was a brand new pair or oars!

THE END

The
Last of the
Monsters

by Philip Steele

Do you believe in monsters? There is one old gentleman who does. His name is Professor Knickerbocker, and he looks a bit like a monster himself – a friendly monster, that is. He has a thick mane of white hair, shaggy eyebrows and a long white beard. He keeps several pairs of spectacles tied around his neck with string, and he is a famous monsterologist.

One day Professor Knickerbocker announced he was going on a journey around the world.

"Is it going to be a holiday?" asked his niece Carrie. "Can I come too?"

"Oh, you can come," replied the Professor. "But you must understand that this is a *scientific* expedition. I am going to search for the Scaly Scalliwags!"

"What on earth are they?" asked Carrie.

"Monsters!" said the Professor, darkly.

"But surely monsters and dragons only exist in books?" said Carrie. But the Professor shook his head.

"Long ago," he said, "there were all kinds of monsters in the world. There was the Abominable Snowman and his relatives the Greater Hairy Bigfoot and the Lesser Spotted Yeti. Then there was the Sabre-Toothed Weevil, the dreaded Nasti-Nasti and the common or garden Wibbly-Wobbly. Today, alas, there are no monsters left – with the *possible* exception of the Scaly Scalliwag from Outer Korkovia! Some very strange footprints have been discovered in the jungle there."

"But *why* aren't there any monsters left?" asked Carrie. She knew the Professor could never resist answering a question, even if it was time for her to go to bed!

"Well my dear, that is a sad story. The monsters were harmless enough, but the trouble was that people were always picking fights with them. At one time no self-respecting princess could get married unless her young man had first killed a monster, or a giant, or a dragon. The last few monsters had to hide away in caves and lakes, and all sorts of uncomfortable places."

"Which were the *scariest* monsters?" asked Carrie.

"Hmmm... Time for bed," said the Professor. "We must pack first thing in the morning."

The very next day Carrie and Professor Knickerbocker set out for the airport. Carrie had a neat little backpack, and the Professor had an ancient suitcase tied up with straps. Sticking out of it were butterfly nets and

umbrellas, tent pegs and bootlaces – and what looked like a very strange trombone! The people at the airport gave him some funny looks until they heard it was the famous Professor Knickerbocker. Then they waved him on to the plane.

Soon the plane took off, and within eight hours they were in the tropics! They then had to go on a long train ride over the mountains, across a desert on camels and *then* up a river full of crocodiles. It took them a whole month to reach the jungles of Korkovia!

"Where are the monsters, then?" asked Carrie when they got there. She was feeling hot and bothered.

"Our search has only just begun," replied the Professor. "Deep in the jungle there is a great cliff full of deep tunnels and potholes. It is there that the footprints were seen."

So off they set through the thick, thick jungle. They passed beautiful waterfalls and swamps full of squirming snakes. At last they came to the foot of the great cliffs. Aha! There were the footprints all right! Great claw marks led across soft mud into the depths of a dark tunnel.

"I hope we haven't got to go in there," said Carrie with a shiver.

"Not if my plan works out!" said the Professor. He rummaged in his suitcase and brought out the strange-looking trombone. Raising it to his lips, he puffed out his cheeks and blew till he was red in the face.

Broop-broop-brarrrrrp! Broop-broop-braaaaarrrrp! Broop-BRAAAAAAAARRRP! The noise echoed around the cliffs. There was a moment's silence, and then a reply came from the darkest tunnel:

Broop-broop-braaaAAAARRRRRRP!

Out skipped a Scaly Scalliwag, blinking in the sun.
He had long woolly hair, green scaly legs and a nose
shaped like a trumpet, which made the strange sound.

"A Scaly Scalliwag!" breathed the Professor. "Just
fancy that!"

"You tricked me!" cried the monster. "I thought it was
another scalliwag! I was so looking forward to a chat!"

"Good heavens!" said Professor Knickerbocker.
"You understand human speech!"

"Of course I do. I learnt it at Scalliwag School,
about four hundred years ago."

"My, oh my!" said the professor scribbling notes.
"Now tell me, where do the other scalliwags live?"

"Other scalliwags? What other scalliwags? I am the
last of my kind," said the monster, and a large tear
rolled down his cheek. "Fifty years ago I fell asleep at a
party and when I woke up, the tunnel was empty. All
the other scalliwags had gone. They're probably as dead
as dodos, for I've never seen them again. Boo-hoo!"

"Oh, you poor old scalliwag," said Carrie. And she
reached up and patted him on the back.

"Do you mind if I ask you some questions?" said
the Professor briskly.

"Oh, all right, why not?" said the scalliwag. So for
the rest of that day they sat there by the cliffs, while the
Professor asked questions like, "Did your grandmother
have orange spots?" and "What do you like for breakfast?"
Soon they were all the best of friends. When it was time
for them to go, the Scaly Scalliwag cleared his throat.

"Ahem...Er...Do you think I could come home with
you and live in your country?"

The Professor looked at his niece, and she whispered

something. Then the Professor held out his hand.

"Scalliwag," he said, "we'll ship you home in a crate. You won't mind that, will you?"

Mind it? The Scaly Scalliwag jumped for joy.

Near Professor Knickerbocker's home in the city is the entrance to an underground railway station. One dark night in autumn he and Carrie led an excited Scaly Scalliwag down the escalator and into the tunnel. There, in a deep, dark siding, the monster happily made his home. He wasn't lonely any more. He could see trains going by and listen to the noisy crowds. Sometimes he pulled faces through the train windows, but the Professor told him to stop or he would cause an accident. He still lives down there to this day, or so I'm told.

And according to Carrie, Professor Knickerbocker just might have some good news in store for the monster. He thinks he has traced some other Scaly Scalliwags living in the Mountains of Mombo. She's keeping her fingers crossed. Are you?

THE END

A
Stitch
in Time

by Sue Seddon

There was once a young princess called Kate. She lived with her parents and her brothers in a beautiful, high-towered palace set on the side of a hill above a wide silver river. In the mornings, Kate learned to play music and dance in the Great Hall. In the afternoons, she went to her grandmother's private rooms, with their huge arched windows that looked down over the green palace gardens to the glittering river, and she learned to sew.

Kate's grandmother sewed the most wonderful embroideries anyone had ever seen. They were fantastic pictures in silk and wool, of flowery gardens, splendid gods and goddesses, handsome knights and extraordinary monsters. The embroideries hung all over the palace and people came from far and wide to see them. They

were so life-like that many people believed that they must be magic.

Kate longed to sew as beautifully as her grandmother. She had spent hours studying the embroideries – and she had noticed a very strange thing. Her grandmother never completely finished the figures in her embroideries. In each case, a couple of tiny stitches were always missing. One afternoon she decided to ask her grandmother why she never completed her figures.

"Well, my dear child," said her grandmother, mysteriously, "that is the magic part."

"What do you mean, Grandmother?" asked the princess.

"Come here and I'll show you," she replied. So Kate got up from the velvet cushion where she was sitting, and looked down at the embroidery her grandmother was working on.

It was a picture of Kate herself, but slightly older. There she was, in a beautiful silk dress, with a little crown on her golden head, standing at the entrance to a huge dark cave. At her side was a monster! It had long, curved horns like a bull, the body of a lion and great gold-red wings.

"Ooh, Grandmother," Kate cried. "It's a wonderful monster!" She looked closer. "I can see where you haven't finished it," she said. "Look, there are some stitches missing from its feet!"

"You have got sharp eyes," laughed her grandmother. Then she grew serious. "I have a very special reason for always leaving a little bit of the figures in my embroideries unfinished, my dear," she said. "And it is a magic reason. You see, if I did finish any of them they might become more than just embroideries!"

"You mean they would come to life?" gasped Kate.

"Well, they might," said her grandmother. She would say no more, so Kate changed the subject.

"What's going in this space?" she asked.

"Oh, that's for the prince," said her grandmother, smiling.

"Really! Is it going to be the man that I'll marry?"

"We'll see, we'll see," murmured her grandmother. But Kate knew that it was.

"I can't wait for you to finish it, so that I can see him," she said. "Please may I help you!"

"Well yes, I think you may," said the old lady. So Kate carried on sewing the brightly coloured little flowers at the feet of the monster, while her grandmother embroidered the prince.

They continued to sew together, happy in each other's company. The sun was setting over the silver river, when Kate's grandmother decided it was time to stop. She looked down to see how her granddaughter was getting on. To her horror she saw that Kate was about to sew in the very last stitch on the monster.

"No!" she cried. But it was too late. Kate had finished the stitch.

There was a great blue flash, and the embroidery was twisted out of their hands. It flew up into the air and began to spin around in the centre of the room. Faster and faster it span, like a whirlwind. Then, gradually, it began to slow down and change shape. Kate clung to her grandmother, hardly daring to look. When she did open her eyes, she gasped – there, in the centre of the room, stood the monster from the embroidery!

"Who called me?" groaned the monster sadly.

Kate found her voice. "I did," she said.

"I wish you hadn't," sighed the monster.

"Oh dear, I am sorry," whispered Kate.

"Well, please put me back immediately," he begged.

"I don't think I can," said Kate. "Why don't you stay here with me. We could have lots of adventures together."

"You don't understand," moaned the monster. "I'll die if I can't get back into the embroidery by sunrise." So saying, he leapt through the window and flew away into the dusk.

"Oh, poor monster," said Kate and started to cry.

"There is no time to waste on tears," said her grandmother. "I think we may be able to help him. But we must complete the embroidery as soon as possible. Only then can the monster return."

The embroidery was lying in a heap in the middle of the room. Kate picked it up nervously, but nothing happened. There was a space where the monster had been, but otherwise it looked just the same. Kate and her grandmother settled down to complete it. They sewed through the night. No one else could help them, as only they could break the spell. Sometimes, Kate thought she could hear the monster sighing outside the window and that made her sew even faster.

At last the prince was almost complete. Kate's grandmother gave a triumphant cry as she put in the last stitch. This time there was a bright green flash. The embroidery flew out of their hands and started to spin like a whirlwind.

44

In the centre Kate could just make out the shape of a man. It was the prince! Suddenly he was in the room with them. Kate just had time to think how handsome he was, when there was a happy roar and the monster flew back into the room. It was almost dawn now, and Kate's grandmother looked worried.

"We must hurry, my dear child," she cried. "There is the background to complete – and we must also bring the princess to life!"

It was Kate who sewed the final stitch into the princess. There was a dazzling yellow flash, and there was Kate! The two Kates smiled at each other. Then the embroidery princess joined the prince and the monster, anxiously waiting by the great windows.

Kate and her grandmother continued to sew. The sky was coloured with the first pink rays of the rising sun, when her grandmother finished the last flower. This time there were no bright flashes. Instead, there

was the sound of birds singing and, before their eyes, the room changed into the beautiful garden of the embroidery! Bees buzzed through brilliant red poppies and glorious butterflies hovered over twinkling streams.

"Home, sweet home," cried the monster, as he bounded into the dark cave in the centre of the flowery garden. The prince and princess waved goodbye, as they stepped into the garden after him. The next moment, the sun was streaming in through the great, arched windows – and the embroidery picture had gone!

"Now you must promise me *never* to meddle with my magic again, Kate," said her grandmother. "I will sew the picture again, and when you are a little older, I promise that I'll put the last stitch in your prince and he'll come back to marry you."

And, do you know, that's just what happened. And the monster? He remained happily in his embroidered cave for ever.

THE END

THE
CIVILISED
SNOWMAN

by Deborah Tyler

The magic started with the very special present Paul
Plank's dad gave him one Christmas. Paul's dad
was not an ordinary dad. He did not have a normal
job like most other dads – for he was a famous mountain
climber! It was very exciting to have a famous father,
but it upset Paul at Christmas, because his dad was
almost always away. Paul usually saw his dad then on
the television news, wearing goggles and a woolly hat,
and waving from the top of some white and glittering
mountain.

Paul wished that he too could climb mountains and
have adventures in a far-off, pure white world. He
imagined himself there, where the sun shone down on
a land of icing sugar and the flakes of snow were as soft
and as large as goose feathers. He wished most of all

that he could meet that strange mountain monster, the Abominable Snowman. Not even his dad had met the Abominable Snowman – although he had, one dark afternoon, seen a huge footprint in the snow. Then, one Christmas, everything changed.

On Christmas Eve, Paul's dad left home to climb the highest mountain in the world. Before setting off, he placed a large, round present, with a very solid base, on Paul's bedside table. It was wrapped in brown paper and it had a sprig of holly on the top so it looked just like a big Christmas pudding. Paul was so excited, he couldn't sleep at all. He lay in bed thinking. What could the present be?

Just as he was about to fall asleep, he noticed a strange glow had filled the room. Paul got out of bed and looked out of the window, but it was dark and rainy outside. Then he looked at his present. It seemed to be shimmering with a bright light!

Paul looked at the bedside clock. It was only eleven o'clock! But he couldn't wait any longer. Carefully, he pulled away the brown paper. There, nestled inside was a glass 'snowstorm', the kind you can shake to make the snow fall!

Paul looked at his present in amazement as it began to glow even more fiercely. Inside the crystal dome there was a snowy mountain, with a glittering ice cap. The sky behind it was purple and dotted with silver stars. And whirling round the mountain were hundreds of tiny snowflakes, like a great white blizzard. Paul looked again at his clock. It was nearly midnight. He reached out to shake the snowstorm but as soon as his hands touched the glass, the room was bathed in a blinding, white light. He could no longer feel the glass beneath his fingers and, before he knew it, he was being pulled into the snowstorm. He could feel himself whirling like the snowflakes, and feel the cold, cold mountain wind on his cheeks. Whatever was happening?

The next moment, Paul found himself sitting on the icy peak of a huge, white mountain. It was like sitting on a diamond, and it was very cold – especially as Paul was only wearing pyjamas. He looked about him. Down below there were probably pine forests and wolves. Up here, everything was white and silent. Then he heard singing! Someone very near was happily singing away in a rich, deep voice. The song ended with a couple of "Pom-tiddley-poms".

Just then the singer stepped out from behind an icy peak. It was a monster! It was not an ugly monster, but it certainly looked very odd. It was covered from head to foot in soft, white fur and had long ears which hung down like a spaniel's. The monster had large, brown eyes and a great bush of fur under its nose, which looked rather like a huge moustache. It reminded Paul of his great-uncle Edwin, the famous climber, whose pictures he had seen in the Museum of Mountaineering. Great-uncle Edwin had got lost on a climbing expedition and had never been seen again.

"I say," said the monster. "A visitor!" Paul smiled.

"Hello," he said. "Are you the Abominable Snowman?"

The monster roared irritably. Then he said:

"Hey-ho tiddley-pom," in a weary way. "Yes," he replied. "At least, that is what they call me. But they're quite wrong. Actually, I am not abominable at all. In fact, I'm really very civilized. I read a great deal. I have tea at four o'clock every day and I like to sing in the mornings. I also love chocolate. I don't suppose you have any chocolate with you by any chance?"

Now, it just so happened that Paul had a chocolate mouse in his pyjama pocket. He took it out and handed it to the monster. The monster ate it very happily, politely leaving a piece for Paul.

"That was delicious." said the monster kindly. "In return, perhaps you would like me to show you round? There are lots of lovely things to see. But first," he added, disappearing behind the icy peak and re-appearing with a small white fur coat and hat, "you must put this on."

In the white fur outfit, Paul looked just like an Abominable Snowman himself. The monster took Paul's hand. He had a soft furry paw, like a bear, and his nails were beautifully trimmed.

"Do you live here all alone?" asked Paul, as they walked along the snowy mountain path.

"Certainly not!" said the monster in surprise. "That would be very lonely. There are lots of creatures like me, living on all the mountains of the world. Once, a very long time ago, I was a famous mountain climber and lived down below like you. Then I came to the mountain on an expedition and the snow fairies asked me if I would like to stay and help them. The birds, animals and plants up here all need protecting you know, and famous climbers, who know the mountains better than anyone, are ideal for the job. So, by magic, they turned me into the creature I am today." The monster smiled and his moustache turned up.

Then the monster showed Paul some of the
creatures he watched over – the arctic fox who runs
through the snow valleys of the highest mountains, the
snowy owl who flies silently above the tallest peaks,
and the magic mountain hare whose fur is as soft as
cotton wool and as white as the snow itself. Then he
showed Paul how he gave the snowflakes their
beautiful patterns, and dusted the ice caps with silver
to make them glitter.

"And now it's time for tea!" said the monster, as he
led Paul back to his warm cave.

"I once had tea with the famous climber, Sir
Edmund Hilary," said the monster as he handed Paul
some buttered toast. Suddenly, Paul remembered his
great-uncle Edwin. He stared hard at the monster.

"When you were a famous climber, before you
became a protector of the mountain, who were you?" he
asked.

The monster smiled and picked up a large silver watch from the dresser behind him. He handed it to Paul. On the inside of the lid, engraved in delicate lettering, Paul could just read the name 'Edwin Plank'!

Just at that moment, the watch let out a tiny chime.

"Good heavens!" said the monster. "It's midnight already!" And even while he was still speaking, Paul felt himself starting to grow. The cave began to whirl about him, bathed in the same blinding light as before. And in the distance Paul could faintly hear the voice of the monster calling after him:

"Don't forget the land where the snowy owl flies and the arctic fox runs," it called, again and again, until Paul could hear it no more.

The next moment, Paul found himself back in his bedroom. His present was still wrapped up on the table beside his bed, just as if nothing had happened. Outside, the sun was shining on a snowy landscape. It had been snowing all night long!

Just then, Paul's dad came into the bedroom.

"The snow's too heavy on the mountains," he said smiling. "I got a telegram at the station. So it looks as though I'll be at home for Christmas."

"Hurray!" shouted Paul and ran to hug his dad. As he did so, he realized he was holding something in his hand. There, glittering just like the snow on the tallest ice caps, was great-uncle Edwin's watch. So it hadn't been a dream after all!

When Paul grew up, he became a famous climber, just like his father. And he never forgot the far-off, icy lands where the arctic fox runs and the snowy owl flies. But although he often went looking, he never ever met again that certain, very civilized monster who had tea at four o'clock every day and loved to eat chocolate...

THE END

CECIL THE LAZY DRAGON

by Sally Sheringham

Cecil Dragon was grown up, but he still lived with his parents. Their house was really too small for three large dragons. But it was very neat and tidy — apart from Cecil's room, for Cecil was a very lazy dragon.

"After all," he thought, "why should I bother to rush about tidying my room when I could just stay in bed, reading a comic? Why bother to stand at a stove cooking things to eat, when I could just breathe flames on my food and it would be done in a trice? Why bother to go outdoors when I could just stay in bed all day? In other words, why should I bother to do anything when I could be enjoying doing nothing?"

"What *are* we going to do with you, Cecil Dragon?" his mother would say, sniffing into her handkerchief. "You won't lift a claw to help in the house..."

"Or try to find a job," added his father, his face turning as red as a strawberry. "How can we afford to keep you at home, doing nothing for the rest of your life?"

"And you make the house seem even smaller," sobbed his mother, "always being here."

"You need to be taught a lesson," said his father, sternly. But he couldn't, for the life of him, think what sort of lesson that could be. How could he make Cecil find a job, if he couldn't even get him out of bed?

"Don't worry, parents dear," Cecil would say, airily, shrugging his shoulders. "It'll all work out in the end. And meanwhile, why should I bother to do anything when I can do nothing?"

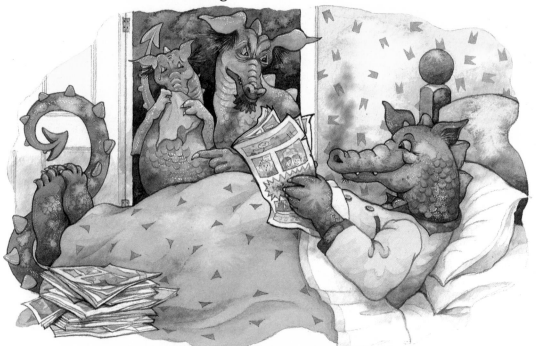

How unhappy his poor parents were!

One day, as usual, Cecil was lying in bed, reading a comic. His parents were out at work, and he was very happy doing nothing.

"This is the life!" he said, sighing very deeply and very contentedly.

Cecil was too lazy to bother to look around. If he had, he would have noticed that the sparks from his sigh had caused the bedroom curtains to catch fire.

Soon he could smell burning. Then he could hear crackling. He also began to feel much too warm. But Cecil just shrugged. After all, why should he bother to do anything when he could be doing nothing.

But this time Cecil *had* to do something. Flames were leaping up all round him. The whole house had caught fire, including his bed and his comic! If he did nothing a moment longer, he would be burnt to a crisp!

"Snakes alive!" cried Cecil, and just managed to get out of the house before it collapsed in flames.

Cecil was unharmed – apart from his tail, which was smouldering. He went over to the duck pond to cool it down. What a sizzle it made!

When Cecil's parents returned from work they found him still wearing his pyjamas, lying on the front lawn.

This time Cecil had really gone too far. His mother was so upset, she needed twenty handkerchiefs to dry her tears. His father was so angry, his face turned the colour of a raspberry. He shouted at Cecil for a good thirty minutes. But Cecil wasn't even listening!

"Don't worry, dad," he said, when he could get a word in. "It'll all work out in the end."

"How *can* it work out in the end?" roared his father, whose face was now as scarlet as a very, very ripe plum. Something has to be *done* first. And you never *do* anything – except set houses on fire."

"Look," said Cecil. "Why don't you and mum go and stay with Aunt Lucy. Leave everything to me. I have a plan. And now, if you'll excuse me, I have work to do."

"I'll believe that when I see it," muttered his father.

But Cecil *did* have a plan. When he had gone to the duck pond to cool down his tail, he had noticed a long line of animals queuing up at Sid Fox's hamburger stall. The animals were getting very cross because Sid Fox was being so slow. Seeing that long queue had given Cecil a very good idea.

Cecil's plan was to set up a hamburger stall of his very own. Above it he put a big sign, "CECIL'S – THE FASTEST FOOD IN TOWN". And it *was* the fastest food in town. All that Cecil had to do was breathe on the food – and it was cooked in a trice! Soon he had made so much money, he could afford to buy his parents a house big enough for at least *ten* full-size dragons!

Cecil's parents were delighted with their new home.

"You've done us proud, son," said his father. And this time his face stayed its normal green colour. His mother even kissed Cecil's cheek.

As for Cecil, he bought himself a double-dragon-sized bed, which he set up beside his stall.

"Why should I bother to do anything, when I can happily do nothing?" he laughed to his customers, as he lay in bed, reading a comic – and cooking ten sausages, four hamburgers and two chicken legs in one hot breath!

THE END